D1089971

Three Little Kittens

by Grace C. Floyd

A Savage Owl Classic

This Savage Owl Classics edition of Three Little Kittens is a remastered republication of the original version by Grace C. Floyd, published circa 1880 Raphael, Tuck and Sons.

Cover and interior pages remastered by Kindred
Published by Savage Owl Press
Dallas, TX

© 2019 Savage Owl Press
All rights reserved. No portion of this book may be reproduced in any form without permission from the publisher, except as permitted by U.S. copyright law. For permissions contact: permissions@savageowlpress.com

SavageOwlPress.com
@kindred.creates on instagram

Paperback ISBN-13: 978-1-7320549-5-0

The Three Little Kittens.

Once upon a time there were three little Kittens, who loved to play and frisk about, and run after their own tails and each other's and anything else that came in their way. One day their mother said, "Now children, I'm going to be very busy, so you can go out to play by yourselves, but be sure you are very good, and don't spoil your neckties nor lose your mittens." Then Mrs. Tabby washed their faces, tied their neckties afresh, put on their mittens, and sent them off.

She watched them with pride till they were out of sight, then she bustled back into the kitchen and set to work to make a pie for dinner. "I'll give the children a treat," she thought, "they deserve it for they are the best children in the world and quite the prettiest, and how smart they look in their ties and mittens!" Meanwhile the Kittens were hav ing fine games,

and they rolled each other over until they were quite out of breath and sat down on a wall to rest. They were very warm too, so

"Where are your mittens you naughty Kittens?"

"The three little Kittens they
took off their mittens,
When they had done their play,
But a Jackdaw so sly those
six mittens did spy,
And stole them all away."

The Kittens did not notice the Jackdaw, and presently they jumped down off the wall and ran home, quite forgetting all about their mittens. They peeped in at the kitchen door, and there they saw, O joy! their mother making a pie, a mouse pie too, which they loved more than anything. Then they scampered off again for they knew mother did not like to be disturbed when she was busy, so they had more games until they were called in to dinner. O, how quickly they clambered up on to their little stools, and took up their knives and forks ready to begin, the pie was baked such a lovely brown and it smelt so good! "Good children", said Mrs. Tabby, "now put your ties straight and smooth your mittens, — but where *are* your mittens?" Then the Kittens looked down at their paws and saw that their mittens were gone, for

"The three little Kittens had lost their mittens,

So they began to cry

'O, Mammy dear, we greatly fear

That we have lost our mittens!' --

'Lost your mittens, you naughty Kittens,

Then you shall have no pie'"

said their mother in an angry voice; "Miaou, Miaou, Miaou", cried all the poor little Kits, for they were very hungry, "Miaou, Miaou, Miaou", but Mrs. Tabby was very angry indeed, and she said.

"No, you shall have no pie", and she carried it all lovely, brown and steaming, away. The three little Kittens cried bitterly for some time but at last said, "Well, it's no use crying, we must try to find our mittens." So they wrote in very large letters, on big sheets of paper, that three pairs of mittens were lost, and that any person who found the same, should have a fine, fat mouse as a reward.

The three little Kittens find their mittens.

Then they pasted these bills up all over the place, and ran home to hunt for their mittens again. They searched for them everywhere; they peeped in the saucepan, though, as that had been on a high shelf all day with the lid on, they could hardly have got into there, and then they felt in the pockets of their little trousers, though they could hardly have been there either as they only wore them on Sundays, and this was Thursday, afterwards they looked on the wall where they had been sitting and where they only now remembered that they had hung them, but no, they had gone and were nowhere to be found. But, at last, in the market, in

the old Jackdaw's nest, they found them put out for sale, and Mr. Jackdaw close by as bold as brass, waiting for customers. Oh, how angry they were! They took old Jack, and they beat him and pulled out his feathers, and though he tried hard to peck, he was only one against three, so it was no use and at last he gave in and the Kittens took their mittens and ran home with them in high glee to their mother calling out

"O, Mammy dear, see here, see here,
For we have found our mittens!"

Mrs. Tabby was highly delighted too, and, said purring proudly and rubbing her paws,

"Put on your mittens,
    you good little
    Kittens and you shall
    have some pie,
Yes, you shall have
    some pie!"

So

"The three little Kittens, they put on their mittens
  And soon eat up the pie!"

although it was a very big one, but then they were so
hungry and it tasted so good. They felt very happy and com-
fortable afterwards until they happened to glance at their mittens
and then they saw that they had dropped some gravy on them.

"O, Mammy dear, we greatly fear
That we have soiled our mittens",

whimpered they, for they
were honest little Kitties
and always told mother
directly they had done
something naughty, and
did not try to hide it.

"Soiled your mittens, you naughty Kittens!,
said Mrs Tabby, and she went and fetched her birch rod, to
give them a whipping, so they all three ran off as fast as they
could. But they were very sorry that they had made mother
angry, so they put their little heads together, and began to think
what they could do to please her. "I know," said the eldest,
"Let's wash our mittens." So they crept back to the house, very

quietly, so that their
mother should not hear,
and they light
ed the copper
fire, and
then they
got a tub
and some
hot water,

The three little Kittens they washed their mittens.

and soap and blue, and they took off their mittens and put them in the tub, and then they rubbed and rubbed, and scrubbed and scrubbed, and boiled and rinsed them until they were quite clean. Mrs. Tabby saw, she did not say anything, but she thought to herself, "I'm sure in all the world there never were such children, they are just as clever as they are pretty." When

"The three little Kittens had washed their mittens
They hung them out to dry,"

The Jackdaw was perched on a bough close by. He looked such a poor miserable old thing not at all like the sleek Mr. Jackdaw

he was when he stole the three little Kittens' mittens. He said to himself "I could very easily steal those mittens again if I wanted to, but no, never again will I do such a thing, for I'd much rather

"I hear a mouse close by.
To catch him let us try".

have my own feathers than other people's mittens." So the little kittens left their mittens hanging on the line to dry, and then ran indoors and said to their mother

"O Mammy dear, see here, see here,

For we have washed our mittens."

Mrs. Tabby gave them each a kiss saying

"Washed your mittens, you good little Kittens, —

But hark! — I hear a mouse close by,

To catch him let us try."

So they all scampered after the mouse, and they caught him, and a fine fat mouse he was too, and though they had eaten such a big dinner they all enjoyed him very much indeed.

Grace C. Floyd.

NEVER AGAIN

THE KITTENS GOING TO EAT THE PIE.

THE THREE LITTLE KITTENS.

DUET FOR CHILDREN.

FIRST VOICE.

SECOND VOICE.

Three lit-tle kit-tens they lost their mit-tens, And

they be-gan to cry, "O mam-my dear, We

sad-ly fear, Our mit-tens we have lost!" "What!

THE THREE LITTLE KITTENS.

lost   your mit-tens, You naugh - ty kit-tens! Then

you shall have   no   pie."   · "Miew !   miew !

miew !   miew !   Miew !   miew !   miew !   miew !"

THE KITTENS TELL OF THE LOSS OF THE MITTENS

Made in the USA
Monee, IL
06 November 2022

17228049R00017